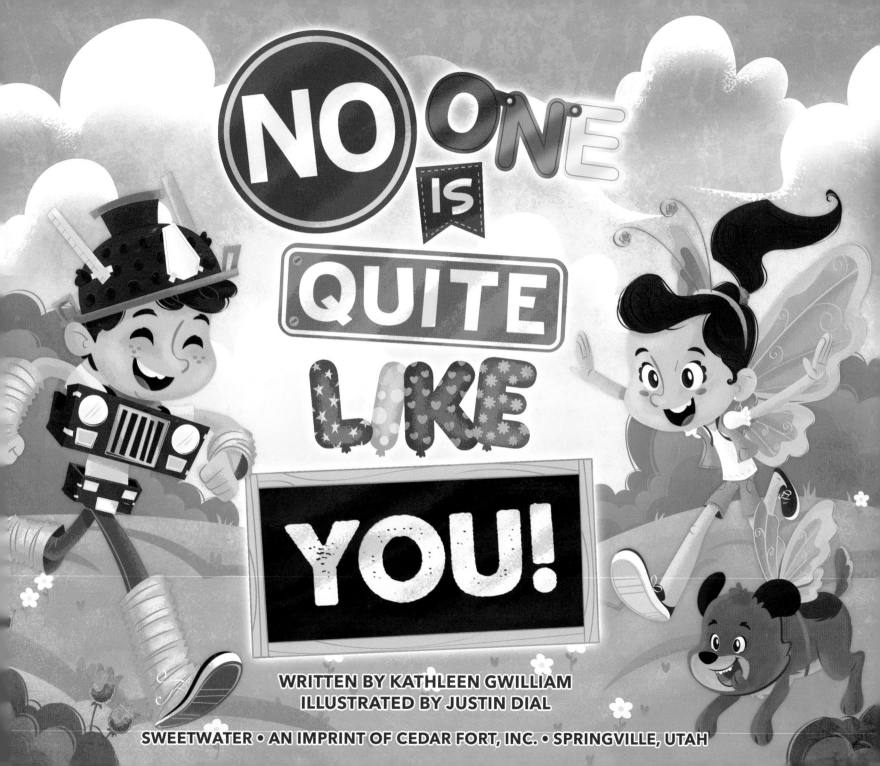

NO ONE IS QUITE LIKE YOU!

WRITTEN BY KATHLEEN GWILLIAM
ILLUSTRATED BY JUSTIN DIAL

SWEETWATER • AN IMPRINT OF CEDAR FORT, INC. • SPRINGVILLE, UTAH

Benjamin can SNAP
Both his fingers and his toes!

SNAP!

SNAP!

SNAP!

SNAP!

Genevieve can BALANCE
A spoon upon her nose.

Gavin is a MATH WHIZ.
His mind's a calculator.

When Evan puts on ice skates,
He's a super-fast SPEED SKATER.

Shannon is the kind of friend you would like to have.
She's PATIENT, KIND, and LOYAL through the good times and the bad.

Daniel's a FANTASTIC CHEF. He makes such yummy meals!

Tess can do the MIDDLE SPLITS.

Juan can do CARTWHEELS.

Lizzy's a GREAT LISTENER. She remembers all she hears.
Nate can hold completely still and WIGGLE BOTH HIS EARS.

Lena is the KINDEST PERSON
That you'll ever meet.

Ollie WALKS UPON HIS HANDS
Just like they were his feet.

Mario can make a SKETCH
Look like a photograph.

Adaline can TELL A JOKE
That makes you
belly laugh.

Jace's dimpled
SMILE
Will light up
a whole room.

If you're
feeling sad
It will chase
away the gloom.

Zane's a great VENTRILOQUIST. His lips don't move at all.

Tamaya PLAYS the VIOLIN,

And Cho can KNIT a shawl.

Cooper makes you FEEL AT EASE
The moment that you meet him.

Marvin RUNS so speedy fast
There's no one who can beat him.

Kylie SHOOTS A BASKETBALL
Clear from the center court.

Rosa DREW UP PLANS and BUILT
Her very own tree fort.

Brynn's IMAGINATION
Makes it so she's never bored.

Kwan mastered
the KICKFLIP
On his lightning
bolt skateboard.

Jane SINGS like an angel.
She has perfect pitch.

Jordan PLAYS the OBOE.

Cora does CROSS-STITCH.

Eve can TWIRL upon her toes,
And BALANCE gracefully.

Kristen KNOWS so many WORDS
She won the spelling bee.

Heather PLAYS the HARP so well
The music sounds celestial.

Cole makes those
around him
FEEL IMPORTANT,
PRIZED, and SPECIAL.

Calvin is an ENGINEER.
He builds the coolest towers.

Oakley has a GREEN THUMB
Growing vegetables and flowers.

Madelyn is CLEVER. There's no problem she can't solve.
Because she's always HAPPY, she makes troubles just dissolve.

Griffin is a SOCCER STAR.
He scores at every game.

Cory PAINTS with watercolors.

Sharese has PERFECT AIM.

This world is full of people,
All DIFFERENT and UNIQUE.
Each one of us is SPECIAL,
From Maine to Mozambique.

There are so many SKILLS with which each of us are blessed.
Do you see and recognize the things that you do best?

You are a child of God,
With talents all your own.

You're valued, prized, and SPECIAL.
Your strengths are yours alone.

He'll show you your abilities,
The exceptional things you do.

God made you just the way you are.
THERE'S NO ONE QUITE LIKE YOU!

To my children, may you always realize
how unique and special you are.
–Kathleen

For my friends at
the Hayden Primary School Library.
–Justin

ISBN 13: 978-1-4621-2340-7

Published by Sweetwater Books, an imprint of Cedar Fort, Inc.
2373 W. 700 S., Springville, UT 84663
Distributed by Cedar Fort, Inc., www.cedarfort.com

Library of Congress Control Number: 2019950921

Cover design and typesetting by Shawnda T. Craig
Cover design © 2019 Cedar Fort, Inc.
Edited by Heather Holm

Printed in the United States of America

10 9 8 7 6 5 4 3 2 1

Printed on acid-free paper